For
Jean

My best to you!
I admire you!
Happy Trails!

Jim & Nathalie

HOW
TO
BE
A
COWBOY

IT'S EASY. . .

HOW TO

BE A COWBOY

A

COMPENDIUM OF KNOWLEDGE
AND INSIGHT, WIT AND WISDOM

JIM ARNDT

GIBBS SMITH
TO ENRICH AND INSPIRE HUMANKIND
Salt Lake City | Charleston | Santa Fe | Santa Barbara

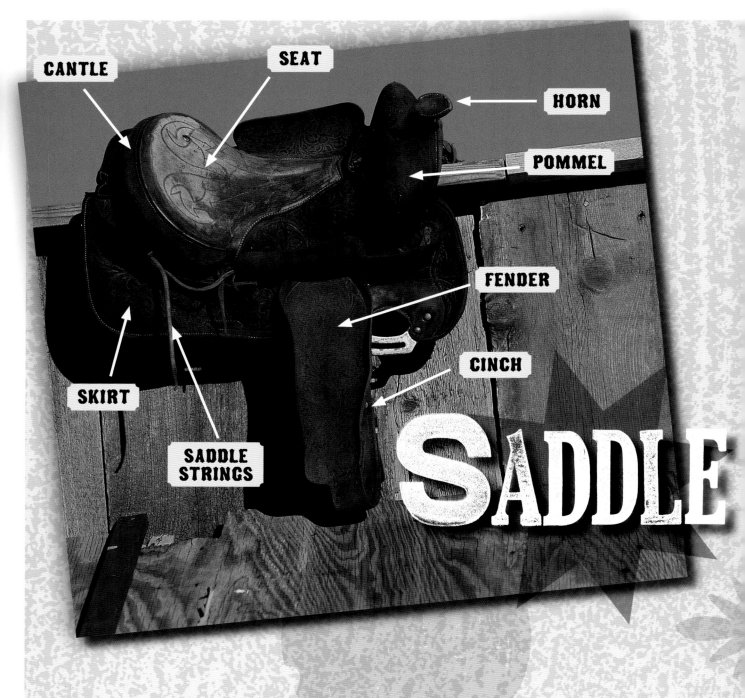

CANTLE

SEAT

HORN

POMMEL

FENDER

CINCH

SKIRT

SADDLE STRINGS

SADDLE

First Edition
13 12 11 10 09   5 4 3 2 1

Published by
Gibbs Smith
P.O. Box 667
Layton, Utah 84041

1.800.835.4993 orders
www.gibbs-smith.com

Design by Kurt Wahlner
Printed and bound in Hong Kong
Gibbs Smith books are printed on either recycled,
100% post-consumer waste, FSC-certified papers or
on paper produced from a 100% certified sustainable
forest/controlled wood source.

Library of Congress Cataloging-in-Publication Data

Arndt, Jim.
  How to be a cowboy : a compendium of knowledge and
insight, wit and wisdom
/ Jim Arndt ; photographs by Jim Arndt. — 1st ed.
    p. cm.
  ISBN-13: 978-1-4236-0642-0
  ISBN-10: 1-4236-0642-6
 1. Cowboys—West (U.S.)—Social life and customs.
2. Cowboys—Clothing—West (U.S.) 3. Ranch life—West
(U.S.) 4. West
(U.S.)—Social life and customs. I. Title.
  F596.A716 2009
  978—dc22
                         2009018451

CONTENTS

THE COWBOY CODE

In sun and shade,
  be sure by your friends.
Never swing a mean loop.
Never do dirt to man nor animal.

— TEXAS BIX BENDER

Lesson ONE

BOOT CAMP

Cattle drives to rock and roll. Dusty boots to couture. The evolution of the cowboy boot from fundamental to fashionable corresponds to the settling of the American West, the birth of Hollywood's silent films starring cowboy Tom Mix, and Roy Rogers and Gene Autry riding across the 1950s television screen.

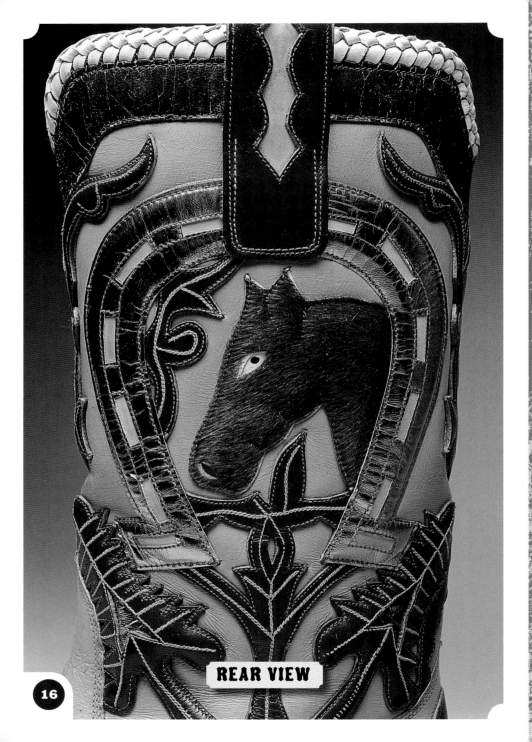

REAR VIEW

16

ANATOMY OF A BOOT

SIDE SEAM
WITH PIPING,
OR SIDE WELT

TOP FRONT
QUARTER, OR
BOOT SHAFT

WAIST

TONGUE

HEEL BREAST

INSTEP

OUTSOLE
STITCHING

VAMP
FOXING

PULL
STRAP

PIPING
(BEADING)

SCALLOP

COLLAR

INLAY

BACK
QUARTER

COUNTER

HEEL BASE

HEEL WAIST

HEEL CAP

OUTSOLE

17

Since the mid-19th century, the American cowboy, the Mexican vaquero, Texas Rangers, and cavalry soldiers have worn high-topped boots as protective gear. Boots were originally strictly utilitarian, and today's museums display well-worn, plain cowboy boots. Because these boots needed repair or replacement as cowboys worked the trail, boot makers opened shops along the cattle drive trails. Over time, cowboys suggested customizations for a better personal fit and later requested designs in stitching and inlays. Even after the last big cattle drives out of Texas ended, cowboys and their boots remained a part of Americans' image of the West.

When Buffalo Bill opened the era of the stage cowboy in his western extravaganzas in the United States (1883) and Europe, he outfitted his performers in dazzling fringed and beaded costumes, and the bright-colored, fancy boots they wore enhanced their garb as well as enabled them to perform rodeo feats such as bull riding and cattle roping.

EASTERNERS

were awed and yearned for the look, attitude, and lifestyle of the West. Even city slickers like New York's Teddy Roosevelt went west (and still do) to experience rodeos, dude ranches, and the aura of towns like Santa Fe and Jackson Hole. Their desire to head back East with their own western gear gave birth to a new industry in western wear that continues to grow.

Boot makers became creative and artistic. Cowboy boots in both tall top and shorty styles became flashier and more ornamental, with new stitch patterns, inlays, overlays, initials, wing tips, collars, mule ears, and outrageous patterns and colors. To show off their flashy designs, boot wearers frequently tuck their pants inside their boots.

In addition to recalling the legends of the West, cowboy boots reflect the personalities of those who wear them today. The ultimate in cowboy footwear today is a pair of custom boots measured and made by hand to fit the customer's form and taste. It is true that boot aficionados push boot makers to be more creative. And it's also true that boot makers push the envelope themselves to design new works for art's sake. Whatever the case, the cowboy boots pictured on the following pages are works of art—some by today's most dedicated, artistic boot makers and others from vintage collections.

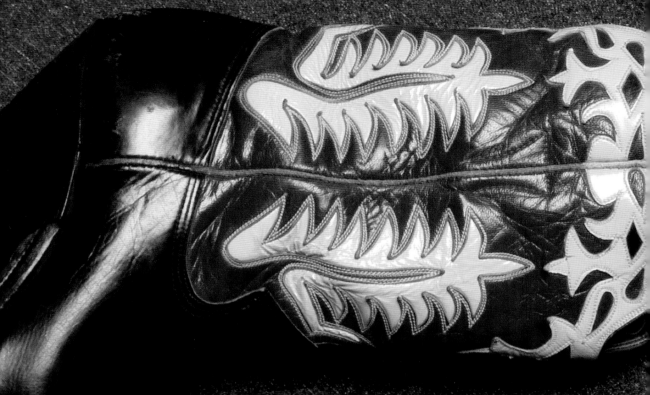

SUPERSTITION

(from dimlights.com)

It's bad luck to step into your left boot first.

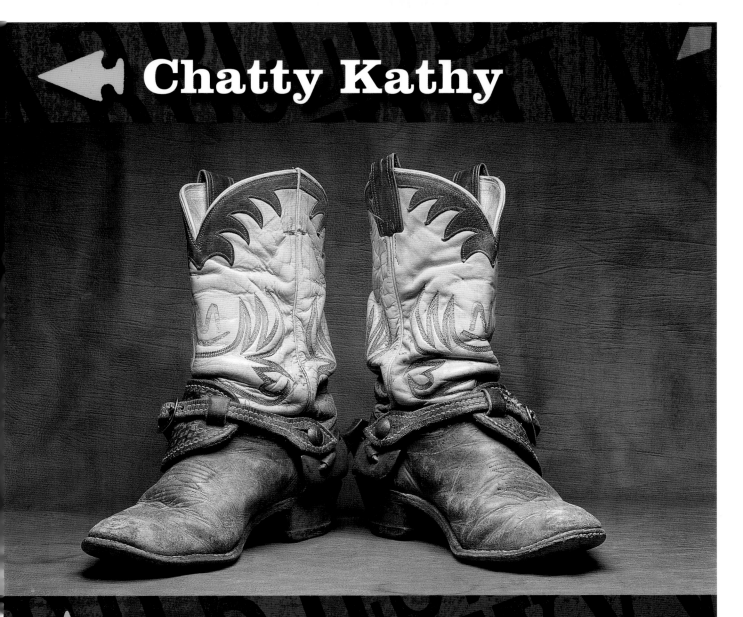

Chatty Kathy

The Strong Silent Type

"People just feel different when they're wearing cowboy boots.

Your stance is taller. You make noise when you walk, and it's a powerful, ominous sound.

Nothing gets attention like a great pair of cowboy boots."

—Jennifer June, from "The Most Expensive Cowboy Boots," Forbes.com

HOW TO
SELECT A PAIR OF
COWBOY BOOTS

STEP ONE

Decide on a general style you want. Are you going to wear them for everyday with a pair of jeans, or will they peek out from underneath a pair of suit pants? For this kind of wearing, a basic black or brown would be a good choice.

STEP TWO

For the line dance floor, you want a little more flash, more colorful tops. These are boots you might want to tuck your pants inside so the boots can do a little showing off.

STEP THREE

Look at the heels and try on some different heights and styles. You'd be surprised at how a higher, undershot heel (angled in from the back of the boot) affects your walk.

STEP FOUR

Choose a toe shape, from round, square, or a variety of pointy ones. If you'll be kicking cow pies in the pasture, you probably don't want arrow-slim pointy. And keep in mind that a pointy toe will add about an inch to the length of the boot, because your toes stop before the point does.

STEP FIVE

What kind of leather suits your personality? Choose your material from tough cowhide or softer calfskin if you want to be a regular cowboy. But if you have a bit of the exotic in you, alligator, elephant hide or ostrich might be just the thing.

STEP SIX

Determine how much you want to pay. Prices of cowboy boots run the range from $150 for lesser quality to thousands of bucks for a custom-made pair. If your budget is $500 or under, you're an off-the-rack shopper. If you can spend $1,500 and up—*way up*—you might consider a custom boot maker.

STEP SEVEN

Try on the boot. It should be tight enough that you struggle a bit pulling it on. When your foot slips into the shoe, it should still be snug but you should be able to wiggle your toes. Walk around in the boots a couple minutes. If they hurt or pinch, or if your foot goes to sleep, try another pair. Keep trying until you find the fit that's perfect for your foot.

Once you own the boots, wear them confidently. They'll put a little swagger in your walk, and that alone will tell everybody that you're a confident cowboy.

FLUTTERBY

YEE-HAW

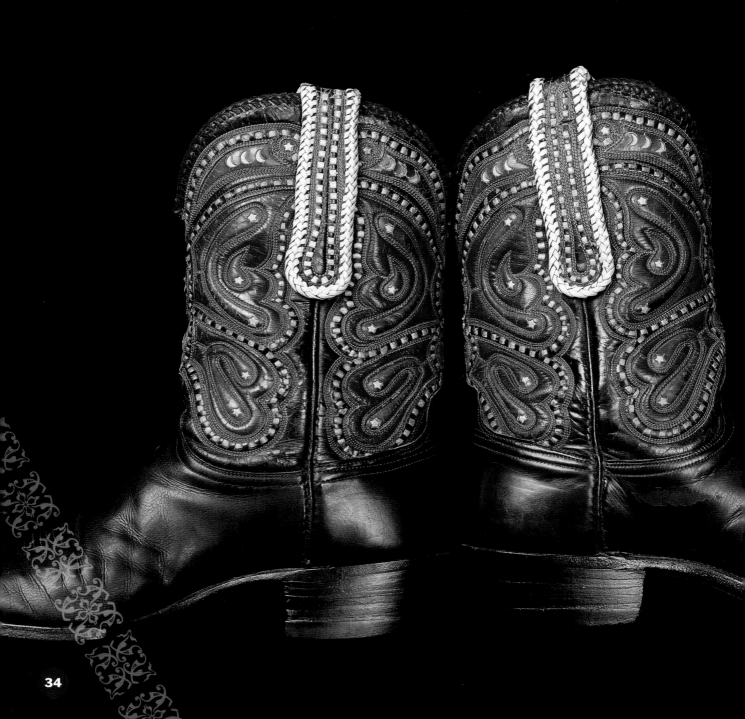

DON'T SQUAT

WITH YOUR SPURS ON.

—TEXAS BIX BENDER

EXPENSIVE COWBOY BOOTS

When someone orders a pair of custom boots, it usually takes a number of months before their order is filled. The reason? Making boots by hand is time-consuming work, and the fancier the design, the longer it takes.

A basic pair of dress boots with foxing on the toe, a few rows of stitching and a simple overlay or inlay on the shaft might take the boot maker only about a hundred hours to complete, though how long you have to wait for them also depends on how many orders are ahead of yours. But once you cross into the realm of complicated overlays and inlays, leather carving and dying, those hundred hours can easily double or triple.

Such is the case with this extravagant pair of hand-carved boots tracing the history of Mexico. Tres Outlaws in El Paso, Texas, was the genius and craftsmanship behind them. It took about 100 hours to create the intricate design and another 500 hours to execute the hand carving, coloring and dying that resulted in a very expensive pair of cowboy boots. (And when you count the cost of life experience, ages of development, sacrifice, war and commerce that gave the boots their historical foundation—this price is unlikely to be topped). Oh—the inlaid historical gold coins cost a cool $18 grand. Total for the pair: $75,000!

PURTY BOOTS

LIKE FATHER, LIKE SON

"COWBOY BOOTS...

...are the only socially respectable way for men to wear high heels and bright colors.

—LISA SORRELL, CUSTOM BOOT MAKER
from "The Most Expensive Cowboy Boots," Forbes.com

Well-loved companions

Cowboy Curio

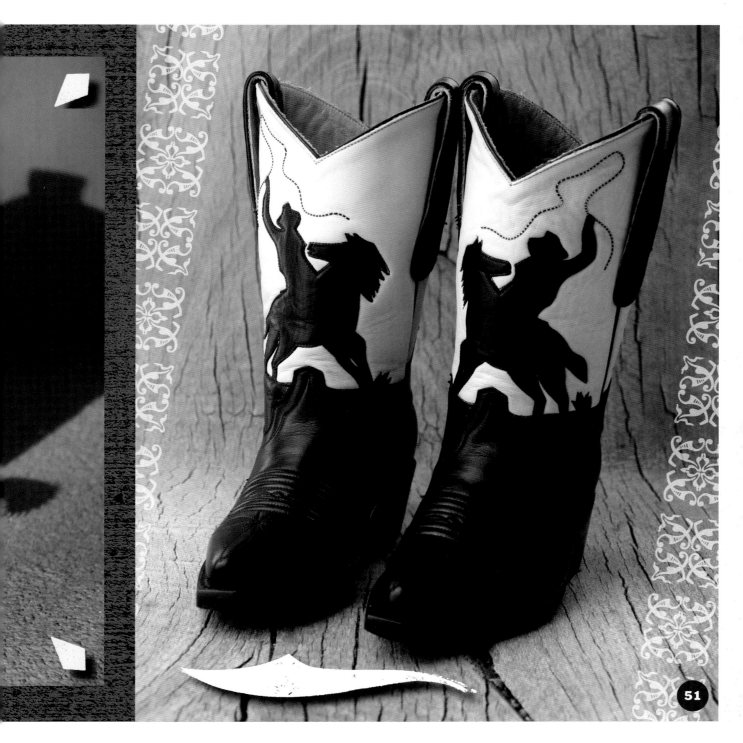

Lesson TWO

THE  SHIRT

Swap a few buttons for snaps and you have a cowboy western shirt. This is what Jack Weil of Rockmount did when he introduced snap-front shirts, not only creating a new style of western shirt but also blazing the trail for a new fashion industry—with H Bar C, California Ranchwear, Ben the Rodeo Tailor, and more following in his path. These became the roots of western wear and western fashion in America. Fashion fades fast, but style sticks forever—and this new western style stuck.

IF THE SHIRT FITS....

...WEAR IT!

For a great selection, and to explore more about the roots of the western shirt, visit rockmount.com. You can even buy a copy of the bible of the western shirt, and the shirt featured on the cover from Rockmount Ranch Wear, the originator of snap shirts. This art deco design, first introduced in the 1950s, is a special numbered edition.

From the era of Buffalo Bill's Wild West shows through decades of rodeos, country and western performers, and rock 'n' roll stars, cowboy shirts and western wear have become flashier and fancier.

LOOKIN'

SNAPPY!

While the bib-front shirt may have been the original cowboy shirt, over time shirt designs went beyond denim into the realms of cotton, gabardine, satin and silk. Rayon gabardine became the material of choice in the 1940s. Designers of western clothing added piped yokes, colorful and detailed embroidery, fringe, sawtooth, fancy cuffs, and, of course, smiley pockets with arrows. In Hollywood, Nudie embellished western shirts with rhinestones to create some of the original rhinestone cowboys, with the exclusive help and flair of Manuel Cuevas, the king of western couture. And Manuel pushed it even farther with more flash, giving style to a beautiful voice. He also put Elvis in a gold lamé rhinestone jumpsuit and made Johnny Cash "the man in black."
And who can forget Dwight Yoakam's RCA cowboy creased hat, skin-tight pants, and embroidered shirts?

The western-style shirt has been worn from the early 1900s to the present by legendary performers such as Tom Mix, Porter Wagoner, Hank Williams, Roy Rogers, Gene Autry, Elvis Presley, Johnny Cash, Garth Brooks, Marty Stuart, Alan Jackson, Toby Keith, Bonnie Raitt, Mark Chestnutt, Vince Gill, and Yoakam, who are famous not only for their music but for popularizing western wear and taking it to the ultra-fancy level. Even star-powered folks like Jay Leno, Matthew McConaughey, Eric Clapton, and Nicolas Cage caught on to the style.

Roy Rogers. Photo from Singing Cowboys *by Douglas Green.*

LASSO UP!

steerin' some luck

Shirts that cost more than a week's worth of groceries

are like horseshoes that cost more than a horse

PURTY FLOWERS

bolo TIES

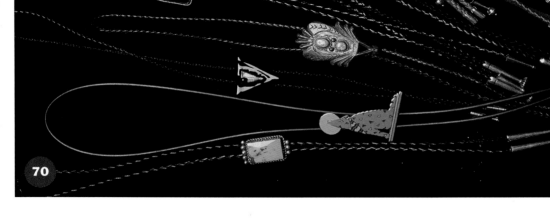

A bolo tie is simply a string (often made of braided or twisted leather) for hanging around one's neck in place of a necktie. The two ends of the string are held together with a bolo, which is an ornamental clip that slides up and down the string to make the look and fit tighter or looser. A bolo tie can be worn with the shirt either buttoned at the top or left open, and women are nearly as likely to wear a bolo tie as a man.

The two ends of the string are tipped in decorative silver or some other material. A Western-style bolo—the slider itself—is often silver and can be designed in any shape the maker imagines—a flower, boot, animal, or star, for example. Bolos are decorated with etching and also cabochons (shaped and polished gemstones). In the West, turquoise is a popular stone for bolo ties.

Both Arizona and New Mexico have named the bolo tie the official state neckwear. So if you don't have one yet, you'd better pick one out for your wardrobe, along with your boots and hat. Otherwise you risk being branded as a city slicker, and that's not the cowboy way!

For the real cowboy, whose shirt eventually became a legend, the beginnings were much simpler.

Starting with a simple cotton or wool shirt, worn every day, it had to survive the rigors of a working man.

73

So he didn't have to wash or mend his shirt every week, he wore leather cuffs to protect his shirtsleeves and a wild rag to protect his neck from the blazing sun and keep the sweat from dripping down his shirt.

And his wild rag, otherwise known as a scarf or kerchief, was usually silk. It had many other uses. He could use it to keep his neck warm, tie down his hat, or as a washcloth, bandage, water filter, or flag, or just to cover his mouth and nose during a windstorm.

A cowboy wears his
bandana for the same reason
he wears his pants:
he ain't decent without it.

—Texas Bix Bender
Don't Squat with Your Spurs On, Vol.2

Sparkly Sidekick

Avoid
FLASHARITY,
FOOFARAW, and
FUMADIDDLE
in dress, speech, and conduct. Leave the Peacocking for the peacocks.

—TEXAS BIX BENDER

Don't Squat with Your Spurs On, Vol.2

THE COWBOY

WAY

FAVORITE SAYINGS

by

TEXAS BIX BENDER

From Don't Squat with Your Spurs On Volumes 1 and 2

NEVER ASK A MAN

THE SIZE

OF HIS SPREAD

NEVER KICK A FRESH TURD ON A HOT DAY

NEVER

Ask a BARBER IF HE THINKS YOU NEED A HAIRCUT

85

TALK LOW, TALK SLOW, AND DON'T SAY TOO MUCH

SPEAK YOUR MIND

 But ride a fast horse.

The quickest way to double your money is to fold it over and put it back in your wallet.

A
SMART ASS

just don't **FIT** in the saddle.

THERE'S A **HIGH COST** TO **LOW** LIVING

you don't have to step in a cow pie to know what shit smells like.

NEVER SIT A BARBWIRE FENCE NAKED

COWBOY LINGO

by

LAWSON DRINKARD

From Riding on a Range

COWBOY LINGO

Just like any other group, cowboys have their own special language. If you hang around the bunkhouse, the rodeo, or anyplace else cowboys gather, you may hear some of these words being used. See how often you can use them while talking to your pards.

BOOT HILL	cemetery
DUDE	city slicker
BROKE	that a horse is gentle and ready to ride
HAND	a ranch worker
BRONC	an unbroken horse, or a horse that, though broke, is still a bit wild
HIGHTAIL	to run off or get away fast
HOSS	horse
BUCKAROO	cowboy (from the Spanish word *vaquero*)
HUNG OFF	a foot caught in the stirrup of the saddle
BUNKHOUSE	living quarters for the cowboys working on a ranch
MAVERICK	a stray, unbranded calf
MUSTANG	wild horse
OUTFIT	a ranch worker's or a cowboy's pickup truck
CATCH PEN	a corral for holding cattle or horses

PARD	partner, friend
RIDE THE LINE	check the fences to fix any that are broken
RIG	saddle
CORRAL	fenced-off area for livestock
SPREAD	a ranch
COWBOY UP	mount up and ride out, or grin and bear it
STOVE UP	hurt, injured, or crippled cowboy
CRITTER	cow or other animal
TRY	effort ("Bill has a lot of try in him.")
CROW HOP	a mini-buck; the horse rounds its back and hops
WRANGLER	the cowboy who takes care of the horses
DOGIE	an orphaned calf
DRAW	a lottery that matches riders and animals at rodeo events
WRECK	a riding accident

Gene Autry and Champion, c. 1937
© Autry Qualified Interest Trust and
The Autry Foundation

Gene Autry's
COWBOY CODE

Gene Autry's Saturday matinee saddle pals wanted to be just like their hero. Gene responded with the **Cowboy Code**, sometimes known as the Cowboy Commandments. They are as relevant today as they were then.

1. The Cowboy must never shoot first, hit a smaller man, or take unfair advantage.

2. He must never go back on his word, or a trust confided in him.

3. He must always tell the truth.

4. He must be gentle with children, the elderly, and animals.

5. He must not advocate or possess racially or religiously intolerant ideas.

6. He must help people in distress.

7. He must be a good worker.

8. He must keep himself clean in thought, speech, action, and personal habits.

9. He must respect women, parents, and his nation's laws.

10. The Cowboy is a patriot.

Photo from Singing Cowboys by Douglas Green.

Roy Rogers' RIDERS CLUB RULES

1. Be neat and clean.
2. Be courteous and polite.
3. Always obey your parents.
4. Protect the weak and help them.
5. Be brave but never take chances.
6. Study hard and learn all you can.
7. Be kind to animals and take care of them.
8. Eat all your food and never waste any.
9. Love God and go to Sunday school regularly.
10. Always respect our flag and our country.

A COWBOY'S PRAYER

excerpt; originally published in *Sand and Saddle Leather*, 1915

by Badger Clark

I thank You, Lord, that I am placed so well,
    That You have made my freedom so complete;
That I'm no slave of whistle, clock or bell,
    Nor weak-eyed prisoner of wall and street.
Just let me live my life as I've begun
    And give me work that's open to the sky;
Make me a pardner of the wind and sun,
    And I won't ask a life that's soft or high.
Let me be easy on the man that's down;
    Let me be square and generous with all.

I'm careless sometimes, Lord, when I'm in town,
    But never let 'em say I'm mean or small!
Make me as big and open as the plains,
    As honest as the hawse between my knees,
Clean as the wind that blows behind the rains,
    Free as the hawk that circles down the breeze!
Forgive me, Lord, if sometimes I forget.
    You know about the reasons that are hid.
You understand the things that gall and fret;
    You know me better than my mother did.
Just keep an eye on all that's done and said
    And right me, sometimes, when I turn aside,
And guide me on the long, dim, trail ahead
    That stretches upward toward the Great Divide.

TOP 20 COWBOY MOVIES

(According to Most-Wanted-Western-Movies.com)

 **High Noon**
(1952)
starring Gary Cooper, Grace Kelly and Lloyd Bridges

 **The Good, the Bad, and the Ugly**
(1966)
starring Clint Eastwood, Lee Van Cleef and Eli Wallach

 **Shane**
(1953)
starring Alan Ladd, Jean Arthur and Van Heflin

 **The Treasure of the Sierra Madre**
(1946)
starring Humphrey Bogart and Walter Huston

 **The Magnificent Seven**
(1960)
starring Yul Brynner, Steve McQueen and Charles Bronson

 **The Wild Bunch**
(1969)
starring William Holden and Ernest Borgnine

 **Stagecoach**
(1939)
starring John Wayne, Claire Trevor and John Carradine

 **The Searchers**
(1956)
starring John Wayne and Jeffrey Hunter

9

Once Upon a Time in the West
(1968)
starring Henry Fonda
and Charles Bronson

 10

Butch Cassidy and the Sundance Kid
(1969)
starring Paul Newman
and Robert Redford

 11

Unforgiven
(1992)
starring Clint Eastwood, Gene Hackman
and Morgan Freeman

 12

Rio Grande
(1950)
starring John Wayne
and Maureen O'Hara

 13

The Man Who Shot Liberty Valance
(1962)
starring John Wayne, James Stewart
and Vera Miles

 14

Virginia City
(1940)
starring Errol Flynn, Randolph Scott
and Miriam Hopkins

 **15**

The Shootist
(1976)
starring John Wayne, Lauren Bacall
and James Stewart

 16

Dances with Wolves
(1990)
starring Kevin Costner, Mary McDonnell
and Graham Greene

 17

The Outlaw Josey Wales
(1976)
starring Clint Eastwood
and Sondra Locke

 18

A Man Called Horse
(1970)
starring Richard Harris
and Judith Anderson

 19

Little Big Man
(1970)
starring Dustin Hoffman, Faye Dunaway
and Chief Dan George

 **20**

High Plains Drifter
(1973)
starring Clint Eastwood
and Verna Bloom

COWBOY POETRY

from *Riding on a Range* by Lawson Drinkard

Cowboys spend a lot of time in the outdoors. Their kitchen is the campfire, their bedroom is the meadow by a stream and their alarm clock is the sun sneaking up over the hills to the east. There is something about this way of life that causes folks to want to express themselves in verse and rhyme that we call "cowboy poetry."

Most of the time, cowboys were a long way from any form of entertainment, so they made up verses and recited them to one another as a means of passing the time in the evenings.

These poems tell the stories of a cowboy's life. They talk about the weather, the land, the cattle and the horses that make up the center of their lives. Sometimes they talk about love or loneliness. Often they are funny, and occasionally they are sad. Always they speak of cowboy traditions and the cowboy way of life.

There are many, many cowboy poets. A few, like Baxter Black, Wally McRae and Waddle Mitchell, have become famous for their work. You can find collections of cowboy poetry in the library. One that is especially nice is *Cowboy Poetry: A Gathering.*

Official Cowboy Poem by Wallace McRae, from *Cowboy Curmudgeon and Other Poems*

A Salute to the Cowboy Artists

Cowboys learned how to ride from their daddies
On some wore-out gentle ranch hoss.
Cowboys learned how to cry from their mamas,
Or a rough-hewn old rawhide range boss.

The Code of the West came from the movies.
John Wayne taught the saunterin' walk.
"Smile, when you call me that, stranger."
Owen Wister taught cowboys how to talk.

Kindly whores and country school teachers
Gave lessons on love and on sex.
Cow punchers got safety instructions
From numerous horse and cow wrecks.

But who taught us "Laugh Kills Lonesome"?
Or be ready when "Horses Talk War . . ."?
It wasn't Zane Grey (though we read him);
And it sure wasn't Louis L'Amour.

But we learned to appreciate sunsets
And the beauty of unspoiled range.
And maybe we learned—call it tolerance—
For culture that at first seemed strange.

We learned hist'ry from calendar pictures.
Yes, we learned how to act and to dress,
For the values, the gear and the costumes
Seeped from canvas to subconsciousness.

Now, ev'ry cowboy that loves this old West
Has a trace of oil paint in his veins.
When the last cowboy's bones are paved over
Your record'll be all that remains.

In bronze and painted on canvas,
So that "civilization" can say,
"This was the life of the cowboy.
He sure gave her hell in his day."

So here's thanks from your friends, Cowboy Artists,
We used your talents as a matter of course
As you captured forever, an era
Of the West and a man and a horse.

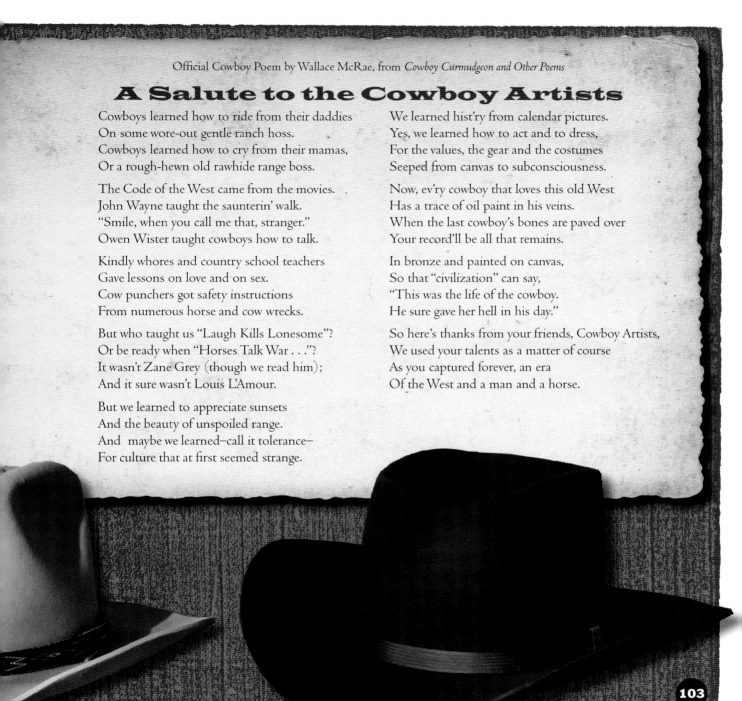

TOP WESTERN NOVELS

From westernsfortoday.blogspot.com,
and in no particular order.

The Daybreakers
(First published of the "Sackett" series of books)
by Louis L'Amour
1960

The Day the Cowboys Quit
by Elmer Kelton
1971

Riders of the Purple Sage
by Zane Grey
1912

Shane
by Jack Schaefer
1949

True Grit
by Charles Portis
1968

The Assassination of Jesse James by the Coward Robert Ford
by Ron Hansen
1983

Blood Meridian
by Cormack McCarthy
1985

Deadwood
by Pete Dexter
1986

Lonesome Dove
by Larry McMurtry
1986

Little Big Man
by Thomas Berger
1964

The Kid
by John Seelye
1972

The Big Sky
by A.B. Guthrie, Jr.
1947

Welcome to Hard Times
by E. L. Doctorow
1960

Sliphammer
by Brian Garfield
1979

Wild Times
by Brian Garfield
1978

DID YA' KNOWS?

From the Urban Dictionary, www.urbandictionary.com

COWBOY STRETCH—catching a quick/short nap during the day. It usually involves you sleeping during your work hours, and wearing your work clothes including your shoes. "I'm just going to catch a cowboy stretch underneath my desk so that I can get some energy for the rest of the day."

COWBOY WALK—A slang term named after the way in which two gunslingers stepped toward each other in old Western movies just as they were about to duel with pistols. "Bob stepped out of the saloon and cowboy-walked toward Steve, the dorkiest gun in the West."

 **COWBOY UP**—It means when things are getting tough you have to get back up, dust yourself off and keep trying. "Let's all cowboy up and get this job finished!"

COWBOY WAVE

From *Riding on a Range* by Lawson Drinkard

STEP ONE:
GET A TRUCK

After his horse, the favorite mode of transportation for any cowboy is a pickup truck. When they are behind the steering wheel, cowboys share one habit that shows a friendly community spirit. It's the "cowboy wave."

STEP TWO: CREATE A STYLE

Cowboys always wave to folks in passing vehicles—whether they know them or not. It's not a big, flashy, full-handed "howdy-do?" kind of wave, but instead a friendly, low-key recognition of a passing friend or stranger. The cowboy wave is usually done by the driver, but you can practice it from the passenger side of your car.

The wave is one-handed and is done without taking the hand off the steering wheel. Every cowboy has his own style and uses his same wave all of the time. Some lift just an index finger, some the first two fingers, some raise all four fingers and some four fingers and the thumb. (Lifting your second and third fingers without lifting your thumb or pinky finger is really hard—try it!)

STEP THREE: GET 'ER DONE

Now, you might think the cowboy wave is no big deal, but if you stop to consider it for a moment it makes good sense. This simple little wave says to another person, "Hello—noticed you today." It's a small act of kindness that doesn't cost a thing, and the world can use more gestures like that.

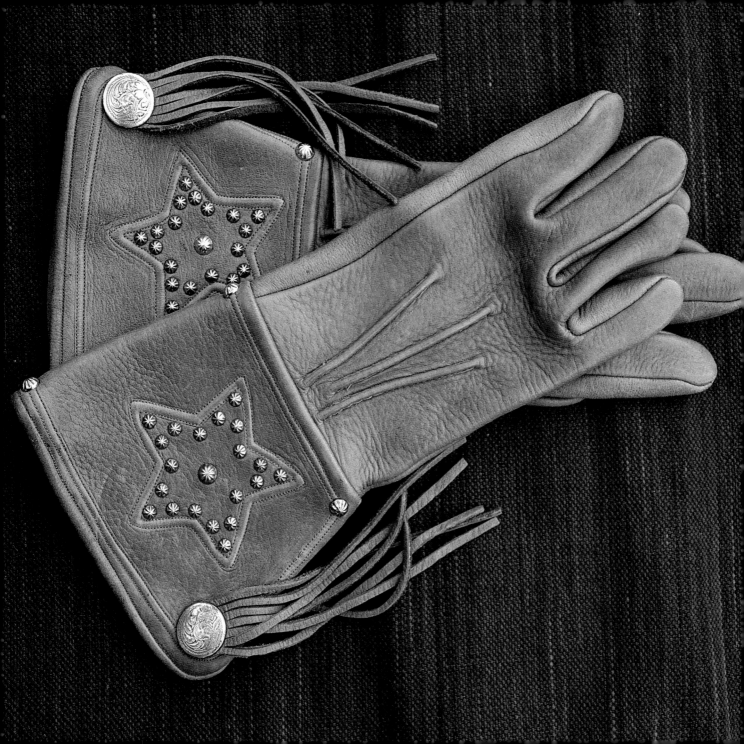

Lesson THREE

DENIM & DUDS

Jeans are the favorite item of clothing across all cultures and age groups. Who would we be without our favorite jeans? They help define and identify us. We're ever in search of the perfect fit, and once we've found it, we're loyal to the end!

WESTERN WEAR
CATALOGUE
SPRING 1959

LEVI'S
AMERICA'S FINEST
OVERALL
SINCE 1850

Prepared for C. R. ANTHONY COMPANY

Photo courtesy of Lynn Downey, Levi Strauss & Co. Historian.

Levi Strauss was born in Germany and emigrated to New York in the late 1840s. He arrived in San Francisco in 1853 to open a west coast branch of his brother's wholesale dry goods business. He imported clothing and household goods from New York and sold them to the small stores of the West. One of Levi's many customers was Jacob Davis, a tailor from Reno, Nevada, who was commissioned to make a pair of pants for a client's husband that "wouldn't fall apart." Jacob hit upon the idea of putting metal rivets at points of strain, like pocket corners, base of the fly, etc. These riveted pants became popular so Jacob looked for a partner, and, in 1873, he chose Strauss. Together they got a patent and started producing the denim trousers that became popular with generations of laborers, miners, loggers, farmers and cowboys. Today Levi Strauss considers May 20, 1873, as the "birthday" of blue jeans, because although denim pants had been around as work wear for many years, it was the act of placing rivets in these pants that created what we now call jeans.

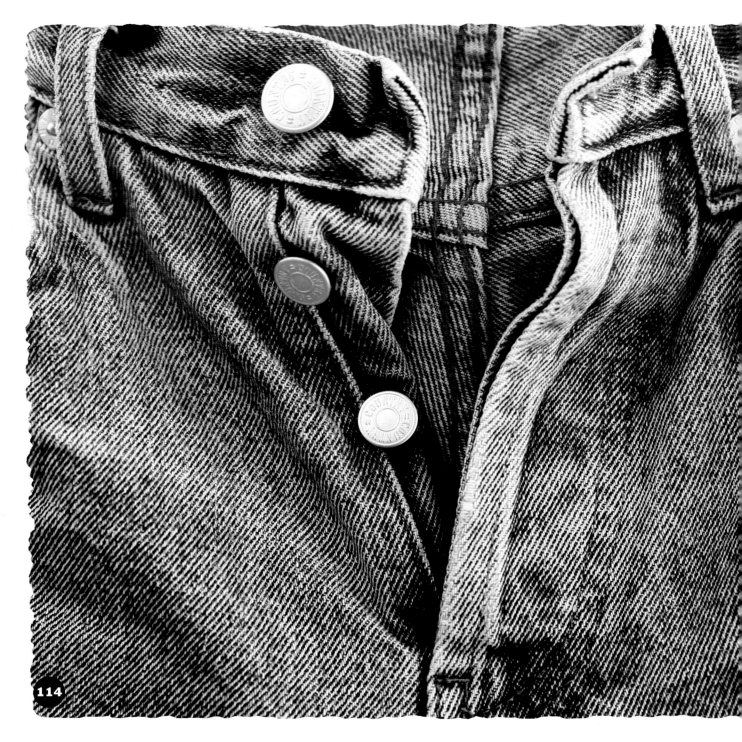

DID YA' KNOWS?

LEVI STRAUSS & CO., makers of Levi's® jeans, has declared the first of May as 5-01 Day, in honor Levi Strauss, who together with Jacob Davis produced the most enduring and popular piece of clothing in history—the original 501® jean.

FROM TURN-OF-THE-CENTURY

cowboy's jeans marked with actual "spur bites" to a denim tuxedo worn in the 1950s by Bing Crosby to modern Levis® worn by rock stars and presidents, the Levi Strauss & Co. Archives reflects how Levi's® jeans have been an integral part of changing American culture, including music, politics and fashion.

LEVI STRAUSS MAKERS OF AUTHENTIC

6092
RODEO SHIRT

2020
MEN'S PLAID

2680
BOYS' PLAID

7068
ROYAL BLUE

7027 — MEN'S BLACK PIPED IN WHITE
7028 — MEN'S WHITE PIPED IN BLACK
Made exactly as 7082
SIZES: 14 to 17. Pkd. 3/12 solid.

6092—LADIES' MAN-STYLE RODEO SHIRT
A dressy shirt of satin finished rayon. A shirt
with true WESTERN GLAMOUR, style and
detail for the Gal who wants real Western
shirts "like the Wranglers wear."
SIZES: 30 to 40. Pkd. 3/12 Ass't.
COLORS: Maroon, Blue, Gold.
Each shirt with contrasting color piping.

2685 — BOYS' COWBOY MOTIF SHIRT
A washable Western figured boys' shirt, made
to tub, that can really "stand the gaff.'
SIZES: 6 to 14½. Pkd. 3/12.
COLORS: Varied assortment.

2020 — MEN'S PLAID SHIRTS
Vivid colorings make this a popular assortment. A closely woven, fast-color fabric, with
hard wearing qualities.
SIZES: 14 to 17. Pkd. 3/12 Ass't.

7068 — MEN'S ROYAL BLUE SHIRTS
Has real "Way Out West" appeal. This highly
lustrous, Panne Satin Western Rodeo shirt, of
American loomed Rayon, is made with beauti-
fully embroidered Long-Horn Steer-Heads on
pockets Has Western diagonal cuffs.
SIZES: 14 to 17. Pkd. 3/12 Ass't.
COLORS: Blue, Maroon, Gold.

**7082 — MEN'S GOLD COLOR WITH
BLACK PIPING**
Like a WESTERN SUNSET! A fine, tough
wearing, shiny satin finished fabric. Piped

2680 — BOYS' PLAID COWBOY SHIRTS
A real "He-man's" shirt for the youngsters.

WESTERN RIDING WEAR SINCE 1850

7041
MEN'S BLACK

6182
LADIES' PLAID

7052
HORSE AND
STEER MODEL

6178
BLUE WITH
WHITE PIPING

7074 — MEN'S SHIRT, RUST COLOR, PIPED IN WHITE

soft as the after glow of a Western sunset
this new velvety-feel satin shirt. A Cow-
unchers shirt that is also durable. With
unded flaps on pockets, and finely tailored
agonal three button cuffs, contrasting pearl
ttons and piped neatly throughout.

SIZES: 14 to 17. Pkd. 1/12.

COLORS:

4—Rust, Piped in White	7077—Gold, Piped in Black
5—White, Piped in Black	7078—Blue, Piped in White
6—Black, Piped in White	7079—Maroon, Piped in White

6178—LADIES' MAN-STYLE MODELS

Exactly as 7074

SIZES: 30 to 40. Pkd. 1/12.

COLORS:

4—Rust, Piped in White	6177—Gold, Piped in Black.
5—White, Piped in Black	6178—Blue, Piped in White
6—Black, Piped in White	6179—Maroon, Piped in White

6182 — LADIES' PLAID SHIRTS, MAN-STYLE

ese Seersuckers need no ironing—just wash
d . . . "That's All". A proven cloth for the
ughest "out-in-the-open" service. Guaran-

2682 — BOYS' PLAID SHIRTS

Models and fabrics exactly as No. 6182
SIZES: 6 to 14½. Pkd. 3/12 Ass't.

6183 — LADIES' PLAID SHIRTS, MAN-STYLE

Construction as 6182.

Made in gingham plaids that are a brilliant
blend of high colorings. Washable and color-
fast.

SIZES: 30 to 40. Pkd. 3/12 Ass't.

7041—MEN'S BLACK SATIN SHIRTS

These lustrous colorings ride high, wide and
handsome with Westerners. Made from heavy
American loomed satin rayon, the large, piped,
half moon, arrow pockets set this garment off
in a class by itself. Note the ultra smart, three

7052 — MEN'S SHIRTS, HORSE AND STEER MODEL

This is a **BEST SELLER.** Made from durable
satin-finished heavy rayon. Has finely embroidered horse and steer heads at base of each
half moon pocket.

SIZES: 14 to 17. Pkd. 1/12.

COLORS:

7050—White, Piped in Black	7053—Blue, Piped in White
7051—Black, Piped in White	7054—Maroon, Piped in White
7052—Gold, Piped in Black	7059—Rust, Piped in White

LADIES' MAN-STYLE SHIRTS, HORSE AND STEER MODEL

Exactly as 7051

J. W. DAVIS.
Fastening Pocket-Openings.

No. 139,121. Patented May 20, 1873.

Fig. 1.

UNITED STATES PATENT OFFICE.

JACOB W. DAVIS, OF RENO, NEVADA, ASSIGNOR TO HIMSELF AND LEVI STRAUSS & COMPANY, OF SAN FRANCISCO, CALIFORNIA.

IMPROVEMENT IN FASTENING POCKET-OPENINGS.

From the Sears & Roebuck and Montgomery Ward catalogs in the early years, jeans have moved uptown. Denim jeans have evolved from the practical and durable to art and fashion. The original big three—Levi's®, Lee® and Wrangler®—faced competition beginning in the 1970s from the designer jeans of Calvin Klein, Gloria Vanderbilt, Ralph Lauren, Versace and Yves Saint Laurent, among others. Big-name designers who wanted their jeans to become status symbols put their signature labels on the outside of the jeans.

From dungarees to designer jeans, the modern cowboy and cowgirl make a splash when they go out for a Saturday-night fandango, a country line dance or a cattleman's ball. Here is their advice: a fancy shirt, bright colors and rhinestones jazz up the outfit. Put on your best hat, polish your buckle, add a jacquard scarf or bolo tie, a fabulous embroidered western jacket and your best dancing boots. But leave the spurs at home unless you really know what you're doing.

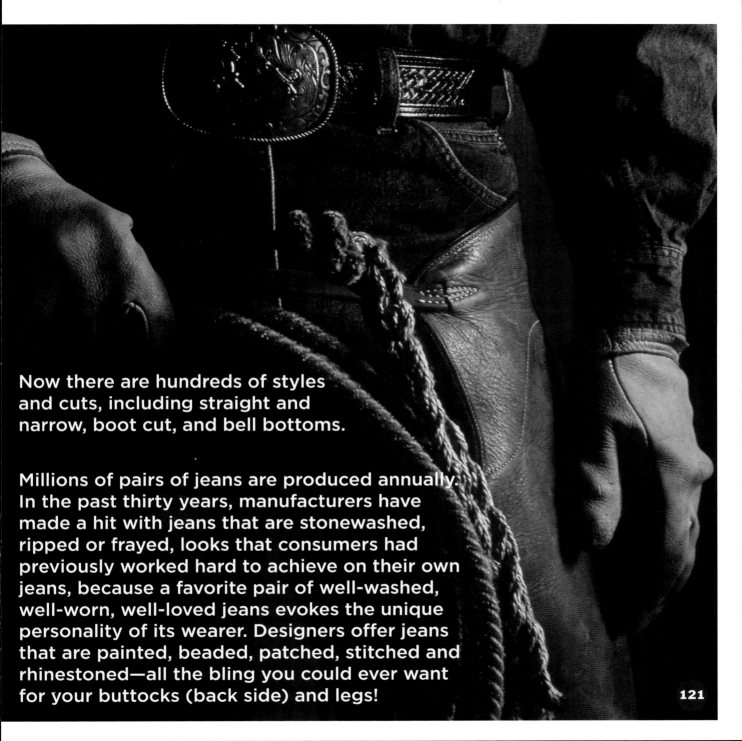

Now there are hundreds of styles and cuts, including straight and narrow, boot cut, and bell bottoms.

Millions of pairs of jeans are produced annually. In the past thirty years, manufacturers have made a hit with jeans that are stonewashed, ripped or frayed, looks that consumers had previously worked hard to achieve on their own jeans, because a favorite pair of well-washed, well-worn, well-loved jeans evokes the unique personality of its wearer. Designers offer jeans that are painted, beaded, patched, stitched and rhinestoned—all the bling you could ever want for your buttocks (back side) and legs!

Roy Rogers.

123

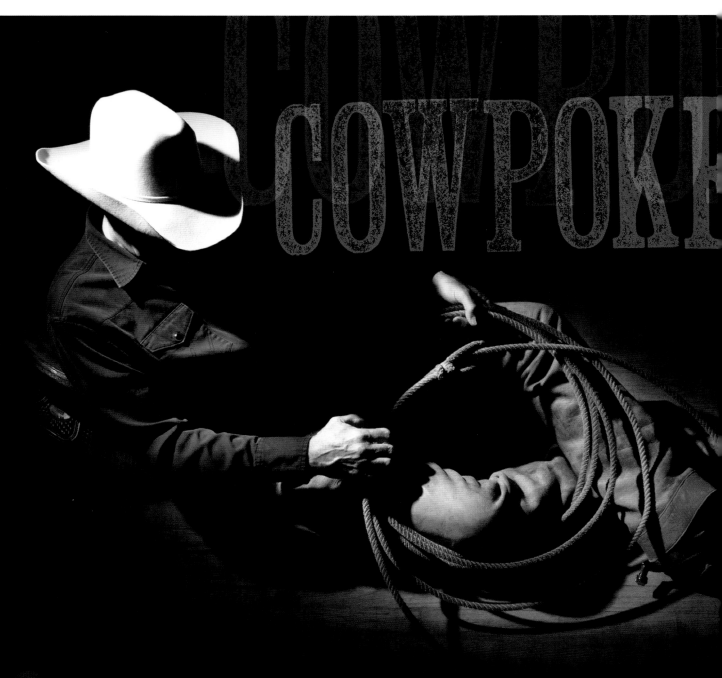

COWPOKE

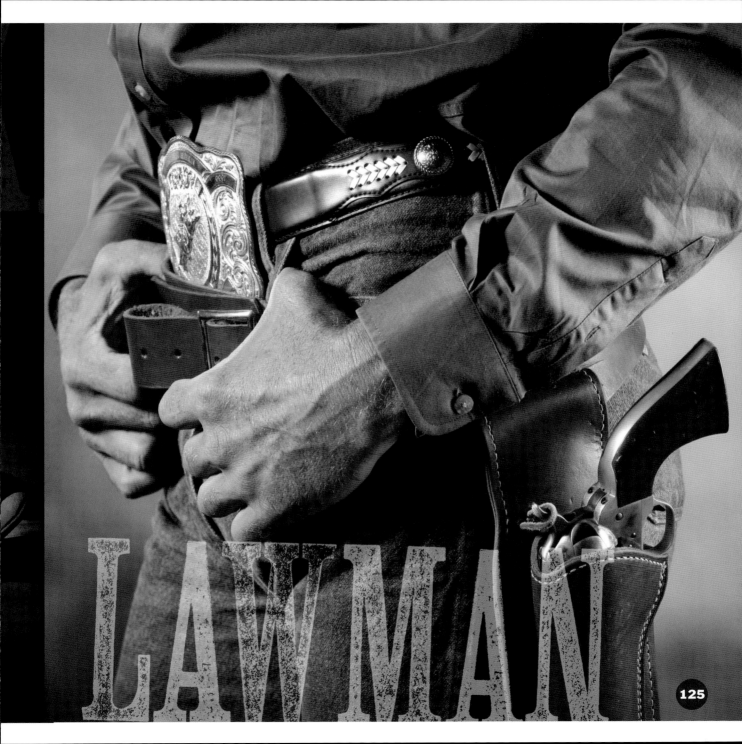

LAWMAN

Lesson FOUR

THE HAT

Since Philadelphia-born John B. Stetson moved west and "invented" the first cowboy hat, known as "The Boss of the Plains," in 1865, this style of hat has protected the heads of thousands of cowboys, shading his eyes from the sun's glare and protecting his face and neck from burning while sitting in the saddle sunup to sundown. He could also use it to fan a campfire or as a bucket to water his horse—practical uses for those ten-gallon hats of Hollywood fame!

In a cowboy hat, you become a cowboy—walking a little taller and striding with confidence as others acknowledge the Western aura about you. They might greet you as "Tex" or, more generically, "Hey, Cowboy!" You nod in response.

WHITE HATS

BLACK HATS

Beaver or rabbit fur has been the most popular material for cowboy hats, and it can be dyed in a multitude of colors. Straw is a more practical choice for the heat of summer.

The cowboy adorns his hat with a hatband of rope, braided or tooled leather or hitched horsehair. Silver conchas, turquoise and feathers add a personal touch. Urban cowboys and cowgirls favor beadwork, horsehair, ribboned edges and bling for a flashier look.

Roy Rogers with Riders of the Purple Sage. Photo from Singing Cowboys *by Douglas Green.*

Through the generations, the cowboy hat has metaphorically become the signature for each individual cowboy and cowgirl. Whether it be LBJ's "Open Road" Stetson, the classic "Cattleman" of Marlboro fame, the "Gus" hat from Lonesome Dove, or Toby Keith's straw redneck cowboy hat, each is a signature style, as individual as one's handwritten signature.

COLORFUL HATS

CHARACTER HATS

In addition to the hat style itself, the way it is worn defines the wearer: whether high on his head, pulled low over his eyes, rolled up in a taco brim, or creased like the "Montana Peak," these personal touches make a statement about the wearer's personality.

Donna Martell and Tex Williams.
Photo courtesy of the Jerry West Collection.

Gene Autry, America's Favorite Singing Cowboy, c. 1935. © Autry Qualified Interest Trust and Autry Foundation.

There are as many cowboy hat variations as there are individual cowboys. Each wearer reshapes it, bends it, creases it, curls it and decorates it to match his own trademark style.

American cowboy hats connote the essence of the American West and may be the most recognized symbol of the United States after the Stars and Stripes.

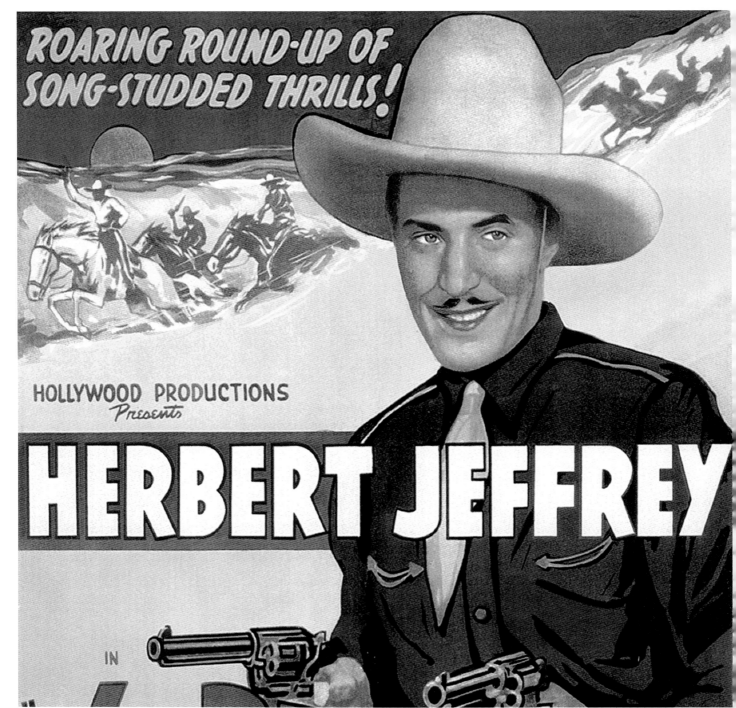

Photo from *Singing Cowboys.*

Cowboy Hat Etiquette

A courteous cowboy tips his hat:

➤ When he greets anyone, particularly a woman.

➤ When he wants to say thank you for a kindness shown by a stranger, such as giving directions to the nearest Wal-Mart or pointing out that his pickup has a flat tire.

➤ When he excuses himself from a conversation with a woman.

A smart cowboy:

➤ Never tips his hat to a man, because that would be like calling him a sissy.

➤ Removes his hat in a theater or auditorium to avoid blocking someone else's view.

A real cowboy removes his hat and keeps it off:

➤ During the National Anthem or when the flag is passing by in a procession.

➤ While in a restaurant (he can keep it on at the counter or in a café where the good old boys gather for breakfast and coffee).

➤ When entering a room of a public building, especially a courtroom. (It's probably okay to leave it on in the library or post office.)

➤ While being introduced to someone, especially if it is a woman.

➤ At a funeral.

➤ In places of worship where head coverings are not required.

➤ While in anyone's home but his own.

HAT FACT

When you take off your hat, you shouldn't set it right side up on the brim, as that will ruin the curl and cause the brim to flatten. You should set your hat upside down, on the top of the crown. At night, hang it on a hat rack or a hat block.

THE X FACTOR

Cowboy hats are made of fur, felt or straw. Originally, X referred to the amount of beaver fur that was in the felt hat, and hats were rated from 1X for a little fur to 10X for 100-percent beaver. Nowadays, manufacturers have their own methods for assigning the X factor to their hats, and it often has little to do with the amount of beaver fur. You can use the number of Xs to compare hats from a single manufacturer and ascertain whether the hat you're considering is one of its lesser quality, medium quality or higher quality hats. But you can't compare Xs between companies, because they don't use the same standards to assign the Xs.

Lesson FIVE

THE  SPUR

The Spanish conquistadors introduced spurs to the North American continent in the 1500s. Luckily the styles have changed since then—the rowels on those early spurs could reach a circumference of six to eight inches! The Spanish influenced the Mexican spur makers, who became masters of the craft. Additionally, many a cowboy crafted his own spurs, with others being made in shops, factories or even prisons.

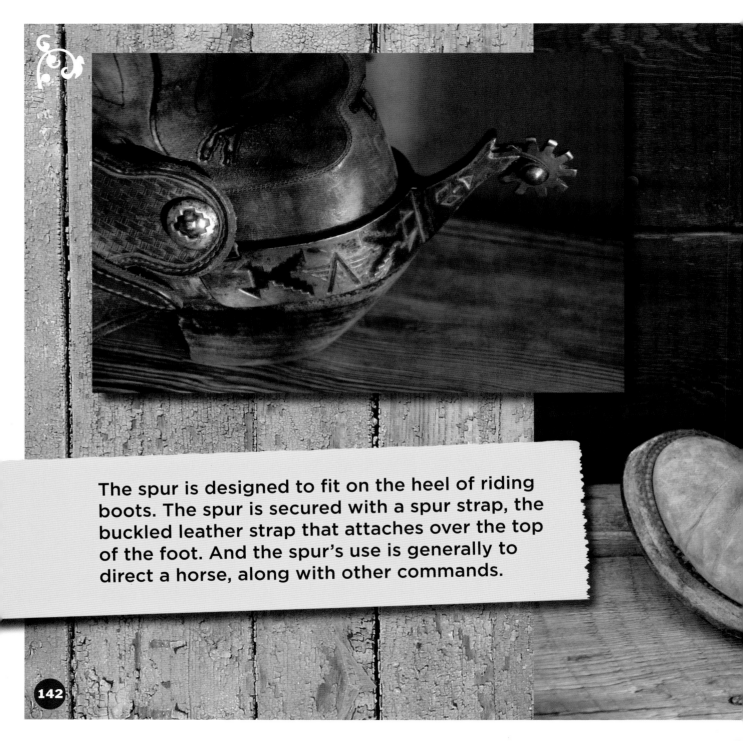

The spur is designed to fit on the heel of riding boots. The spur is secured with a spur strap, the buckled leather strap that attaches over the top of the foot. And the spur's use is generally to direct a horse, along with other commands.

EARN YER SPURS

Like belt buckles, fancy spurs can be awarded to rodeo champions.

In his winning event, he has "earned his spurs"!

Western-style cowboy spurs have rowels, or spinning wheels or discs, on the tail end of the spur shank. Rowels are basically round but can be in the shape of a flower, four-leaf clover or star or just have a bunch of pointy ends. Silver dollars have also been used. Some cowboys attach a pair of jingling pendants known as jingle bobs to the rowel pins to make a little music when they walk.

The shank (the slightly curved piece of steel between the rowel and the heel band that wraps around the back of the boot) can either be plain or have a more interesting shape, such as a snake or the classic "gal leg." On the outside of the heel band is where the adornment usually goes. But also on the button that the spur strap hooks onto. The button might also be replaced with a slot for the leathers. Decoration can even be on the chap guard, which is a small protrusion that keeps the chaps from getting entangled in the rowel.

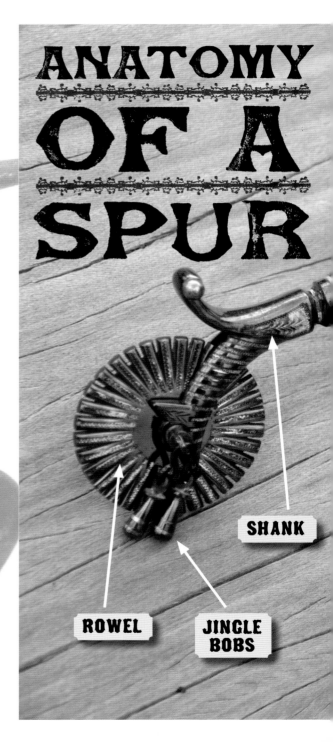

ANATOMY OF A SPUR

SHANK

ROWEL

JINGLE BOBS

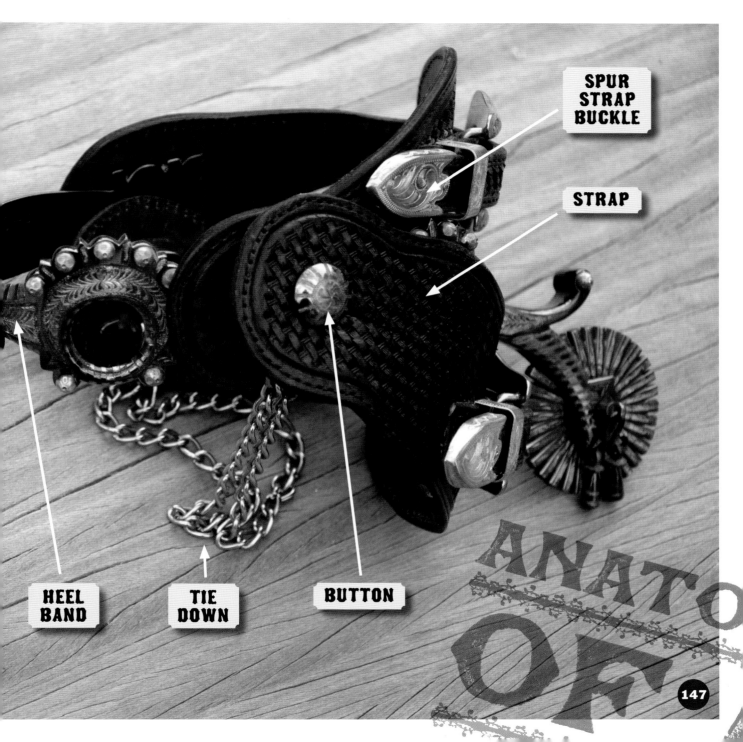

SPUR
STRAP
BUCKLE

STRAP

HEEL
BAND

TIE
DOWN

BUTTON

ANATO

147

Spurs can be simply utilitarian to meet the needs of the working cowboy, or they can be beautifully artistic, dictated by the taste of the cowboy and the skill of the maker. Inlaid and overlaid (meaning layers of metals laid over or under other layers for the sake of design) longhorns, stars and moons, hearts, brands and initials are popular for spurs and for the leather spur straps that attach them to the cowboy's boot. Hand-forged steel spurs can be inlaid with copper, brass, silver or gold and may include turquoise and other precious or semiprecious stones.

FANGIFTED

Spurs are standard equipment for the working cowboy, as integral and personal a part of his gear as are his boots, hat and saddle. Once the cowboy is mounted, a nudge from his spurs on the horse's flank helps direct the animal. Giddyap!

Spurs are no longer merely a working tool but have become collectible works of art, whether they are the classic spurs of yesteryear or today's custom masterpieces.

Lesson SIX

THE  RODEO

Rodeo cowboys live their own lifestyle, have their own culture, and talk their special lingo. Competitors "ride the shows" or follow the rodeo circuit. Each has a specialty event or two: calf roping, steer wrestling, bull riding, or saddle or bareback bronc riding. The cowgirl competitors' main event is barrel racing, an amazing feat of human/equine coordination and skill.

William F. Cody, Pawnee Bill, and Buffalo Jones. Photo from Denver Public Library.

Today's cowboys may wish they were paid performers like Annie Oakley or Buck Taylor in Buffalo Bill's Wild West shows. Instead, they pay entry fees for the privilege of getting bucked around and broken up. They don't make a penny if they don't win their event.

These rodeo contests developed from the 1800s working cowboy's duties, though somewhat modified for a competitive event. Most early rodeo cowboys were working cowboys who daily practiced their skills; then when a roundup or rodeo was staged, they participated to show off their stuff to the other cowboys.

COWBOY

With strength, skill and spirit, rodeo cowboys jam their hats on their heads, grip a rein in one hand and hold the other hand overhead. When the gate opens on the bucking animal, it is man versus beast, danger and brute power versus glory and prize money. For eight seconds, the bull or bronc rider summons all his strength and courage to stay atop the animal while the spectators hold their breaths that the cowboy will survive not only the eight seconds but with life and limb. Many a stoic cowboy has gotten up from the dust, grimaced while his broken ribs were being taped, and then climbed in the chute for the next ride.

5085. Typical Cowboys waiting their turn at Bucking Contest.

COWBOY UP!

The rodeo circuit

today, governed by the Professional Rodeo Cowboys Association (PRCA), is big business. Rodeos such as the Cheyenne Frontier Days, the Pendleton Roundup, the Calgary Stampede and even small county rodeos promote tourism. The crowd-pleasing acts are breathtaking not only because of the dangers involved but also the showmanship.

The wardrobe of the rodeo cowboy is similar to that of the cowboy working cattle on the range, but also derives from the "fancy" cowboy clothing of television and movies. Maybe it's more like the working cowboy's "goin' to town" clothes. The fancy style with brightly colored shirts and leather chaps makes a flashier looking ride. Adding to the bright colors are fringes, sequins or rhinestones, and silver. This is even more evident on women performers, especially the rodeo queens.

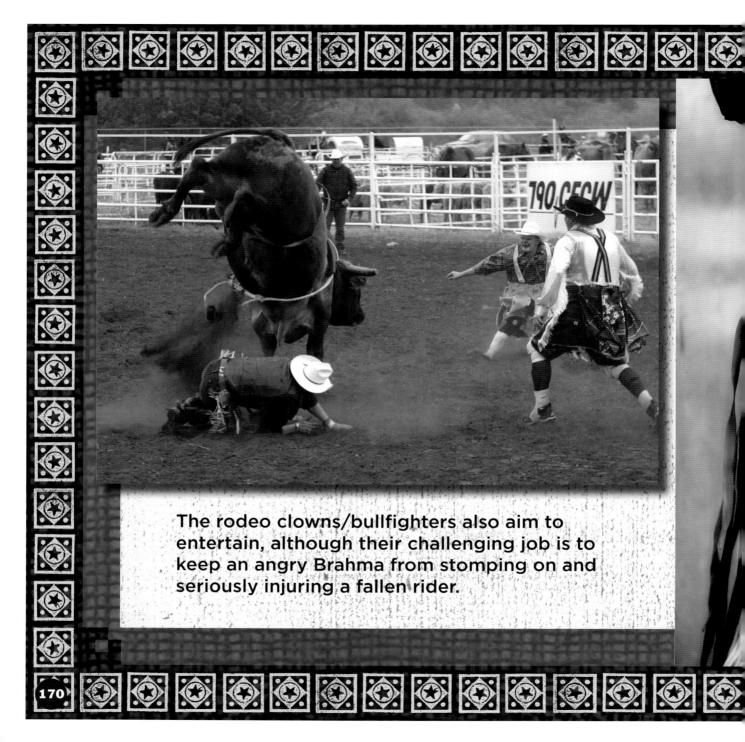

The rodeo clowns/bullfighters also aim to entertain, although their challenging job is to keep an angry Brahma from stomping on and seriously injuring a fallen rider.

Lesson SEVEN

THE RANCH

WEST MESA RANCH

Before the invention of barbed wire, cattle by the millions roamed free in western and southern Texas, grazing the open range. Drovers (and industrious cattle rustlers) herded them north to the Kansas railheads of Abilene and Wichita for shipping to the East. The cattle lost weight and their meat toughened on these drives, hundreds of miles long.

In 1874, Joseph Glidden was granted a patent on the type of barbed wire still used today. With the introduction of this type of fencing, cattle that had roamed wild could now be owned, contained and grazed, and thus ranches were born. Cattle barons developed ranches over thousands of acres, choosing acreage with clean water and abundant grass.

Since a ranch's acreage was vast, it meant that in order to tend to all of it—mend fences, gather cattle, etc.— cowboys had to go on some very long horseback rides and spend some nights under the open stars.

The ranch today bears a remarkable resemblance to those of the early days. Even with modern technologies, the cowboys contend with dust, excessive heat, thunderous rainstorms and bitter blizzards. Their workday lasts from sunup to sundown. The open range is their office. A good string of horses, a saddle and a lariat are still the tools of the trade. Astride their horses, cowboys round up livestock that are straying or in trouble. They brand them. They mend fences. They follow the foreman's orders.

working ranch can consist of thousands of acres. Or a smaller "ranchito" can be more of a home than a business. The important factor here is that, however small, it is yours. Whatever its size, as the proud owner, you think, act and dress like a cowboy. Your ranch has a name that reflects your persona. You have a brand that incorporates your initials or your ranch name. The interior decor of your ranch house probably includes a longhorn skull, rustic log furniture, an antler lamp, Pendleton camp blankets, an antique saddle and a horseshoe—for luck—over the door. Add to that a fire in your massive stone fireplace and you will know that you are "home on the range."

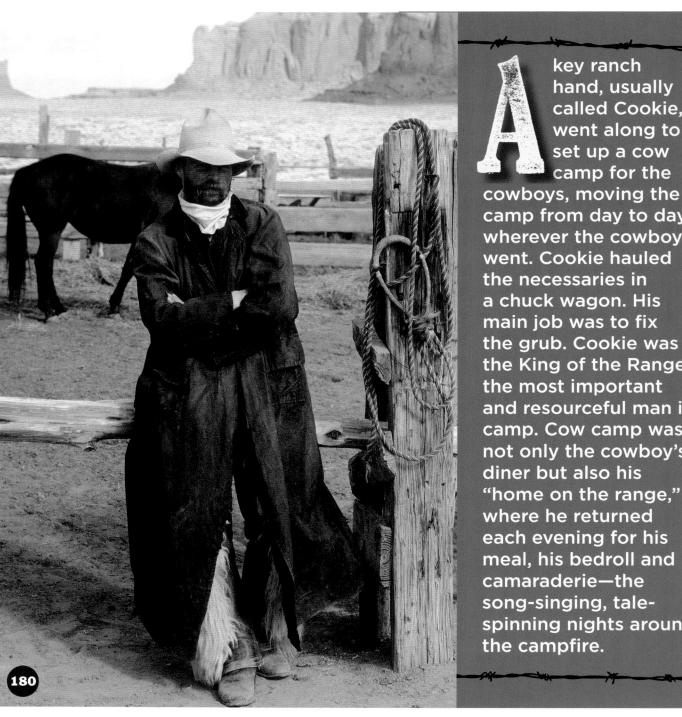

A key ranch hand, usually called Cookie, went along to set up a cow camp for the cowboys, moving the camp from day to day, wherever the cowboys went. Cookie hauled the necessaries in a chuck wagon. His main job was to fix the grub. Cookie was the King of the Range, the most important and resourceful man in camp. Cow camp was not only the cowboy's diner but also his "home on the range," where he returned each evening for his meal, his bedroll and camaraderie—the song-singing, tale-spinning nights around the campfire.

HEY, COOKIE!

DID YA' KNOWS?

From the Urban Dictionary, www.urbandictionary.com

COWBOY BREAKFAST—A leak and a look around. "We were in a hurry, so we only had time for a cowboy breakfast."

COWBOY COFFEE—Making a great cup of coffee in the backcountry is easy when you prepare it the way cowboys have done for over a century. Simply pour the coffee grounds into a cup of hot water and stir. Most of the coffee will dissolve in the water. The remaining grains are then sifted through the front teeth. This is also a great solution for people who cannot afford a $5 cup of joe from Starbucks. "That homeless guy must have just had a cup of cowboy coffee. His teeth are full of coffee grounds!"

THE GOURMET COWBOY

Courtesy of Texas Bix Bender

MUD—Coffee

SINKERS—Biscuits

WHISTLEBERRIES—Beans

HEN FRUIT—Eggs

SHOE SOLES—Pancakes

GUT ROBBER—Cook

SKUNK EGGS—Onions

SHEEPDIP—Coffee

EGGS BRIGHT-EYED—Eggs Sunny Side Up

PUNK—Bread

LEAD SNOWBALLS—Biscuits

GREASE HUNGRY—Wanting some meat

A Cowboy's Best Friends:

A TRUSTY STEED...

A FAITHFUL COMPANION...

A PICKUP TRUCK...

DECORATED OR NOT.

Charles Starrett and Elton Britt.
Photo from Singing Cowboys by Douglas Green.

Lesson EIGHT

THE  MUSIC

Cowboy music reflects the poetry of his days—trailing cattle, thwacking through sagebrush, bracing against howling winds, mending fences and riding in solitude.

Gene Autry on Movie Lobby Card of Tumbling Tumbleweeds, *1935.*
(c) Autry Qualified Interest Trust and The Autry Foundation.

A MONOGRAM PICTURE

TEX RITTER "ROLL WAGONS ROLL"

PRINTED IN U. S. A.

Photo from Singing Cowboys.

Leaning on their bedrolls around a campfire, cowboys shared their folklore in poetry and music. At the campsite, the music of the harmonica or jaw harp might accompany an old ballad or a brisk and lively boot-stomping jig. Occasionally a cowboy camp might hear the music of a fiddle or banjo. And an enterprising musician might easily become a drummer by turning a bucket upside down and tapping out the rhythm with a utensil or a stick—rounding out a sort of frontier band!

Hard-luck stories (and humorous ones!), adventures, tall tales and lost loves were common themes. Friends—human and equine—who died tragic deaths on the prairie were memorialized in song. Trail drives, stampedes and outlaws were also reflected in the lyrics. A cowboy's sense of humor was apparent in songs that poked fun at himself, and, with no ladies present, the language could be colorful, lusty or profane!

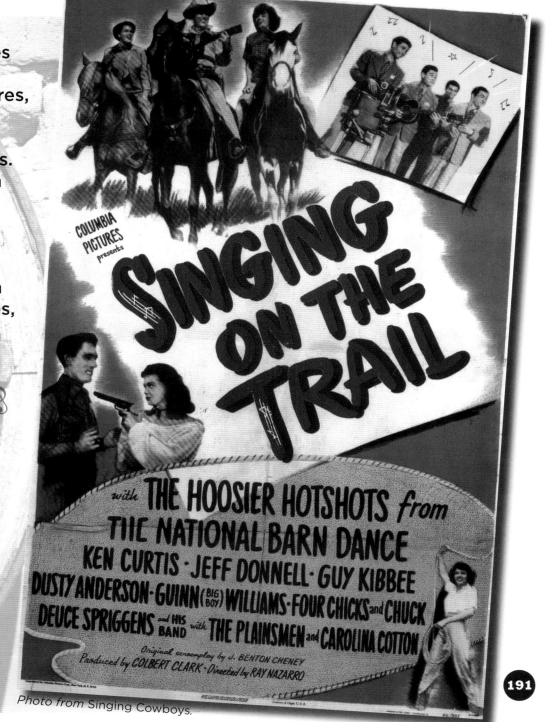

COLUMBIA PICTURES presents

SINGING ON THE TRAIL

with THE HOOSIER HOTSHOTS from THE NATIONAL BARN DANCE
KEN CURTIS · JEFF DONNELL · GUY KIBBEE
DUSTY ANDERSON · GUINN (BIG BOY) WILLIAMS · FOUR CHICKS and CHUCK
DEUCE SPRIGGENS and HIS BAND with THE PLAINSMEN and CAROLINA COTTON

Original screenplay by J. BENTON CHENEY
Produced by COLBERT CLARK · Directed by RAY NAZARRO

Photo from Singing Cowboys.

Photo from Singing Cowboys.

With film and television westerns of the 1930s, '40s and '50s, the popularity of all things cowboy, including music, exploded. Everybody knew the singing cowboys—Roy Rogers, Gene Autry, Rex Allen, Hank Williams, Tex Ritter, Bob Wills, Marty Robbins and Sons of the Pioneers. They popularized old cowboy verses and ballads and also wrote their own signature lyrics and melodies.

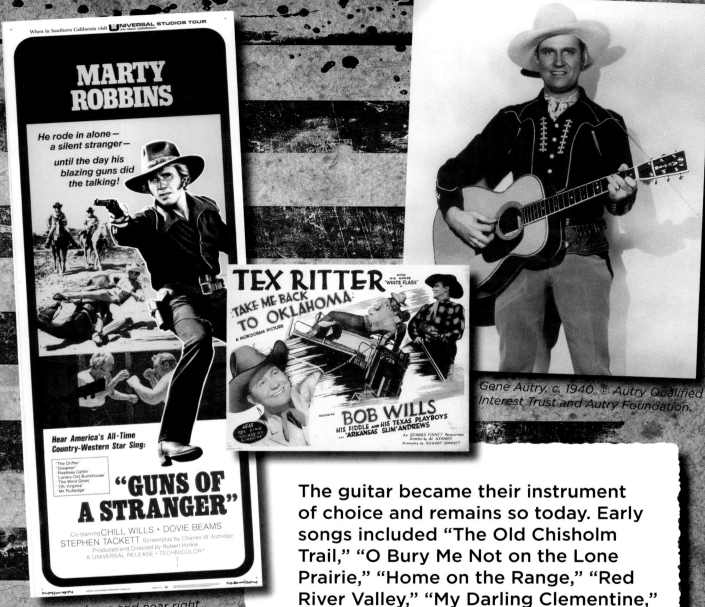

When in Southern California visit UNIVERSAL STUDIOS TOUR AN MCA COMPANY

MARTY ROBBINS

He rode in alone —
a silent stranger —

until the day his
blazing guns did
the talking!

Hear America's All-Time
Country-Western Star Sing:

"The Drifter"
"Dreamer"
"Restless Cattle"
"Lonely Old Bunkhouse"
"The Wind Goes"
"Oh, Virginia"
"Mr. Rutledge"

"GUNS OF A STRANGER"

Co-starring CHILL WILLS · DOVIE BEAMS
STEPHEN TACKETT Screenplay by Charles W. Aldridge
Produced and Directed by Robert Hinkle
A UNIVERSAL RELEASE · TECHNICOLOR®

Photos above and near right from Singing Cowboys.

TEX RITTER WITH HIS HORSE "WHITE FLASH"
TAKE ME BACK TO OKLAHOMA
A MONOGRAM PICTURE

HEAR TEX SING "YOU ARE MY SUNSHINE"

FEATURING **BOB WILLS**
HIS FIDDLE AND HIS TEXAS PLAYBOYS
WITH "ARKANSAS SLIM" ANDREWS

An EDWARD FINNEY Production
Directed by AL HERMAN
Screenplay by ROBERT EMMETT

Gene Autry, c. 1940. © Autry Qualified Interest Trust and Autry Foundation.

The guitar became their instrument of choice and remains so today. Early songs included "The Old Chisholm Trail," "O Bury Me Not on the Lone Prairie," "Home on the Range," "Red River Valley," "My Darling Clementine," "Home Sweet Home," and "Git Along, Little Dogies."

BING CROSBY was a Singing Cowboy!

Photo from *Singing Cowboys.*

BING CROSBY'S OUTSTANDING HIT

I'm An Old Cowhand

(FROM THE RIO GRANDE)

Photo from Singing Cowboys.

Includes Instructional CD

World-Famous Yahooer, WYLIE GUSTAFSON

How to YODEL

Lessons to Tickle Your

Today there are still many singers performing cowboy music and entertaining audiences in performance halls and gymnasiums, such as Riders in the Sky and Sons of the Pioneers, singing the old classics and writing some new cowboy western songs of their own. There's Wylie Gustafson making audiences happy with his singing, yodeling and contemporary sound, and revered singers the likes of Ian Tyson and Don Edwards pleasing crowds with their mellow tones. But in the mainstream, country & western music is a widely popular outgrowth of the original cowboy music. Stars such as Garth Brooks, Toby Keith, George Strait, Dwight Yoakam, Marty Stuart, Randy Travis and Brooks & Dunn wow their millions of fans with music ranging from pure country to redneck to rockabilly.

Photo courtesy of *Riders in the Sky.*

RIDERS IN THE SKY

No matter how old you are, cowboy country music is good medicine for a mood change, whether you're tapping your toes to the rhythm, singing along to your MP3 player or gliding across the dance floor in a classic two-step to the sound of good honky-tonk or a Western fiddle band!

Charles **STARRETT**

THE **COLORADO TRAIL** A COLUMBIA PICTURE

Photo from Singing Cowboys.

199

Fuzzy Knight, Tex Ritter and friends. Photo from Singing Cowboys.

Lesson NINE

THE 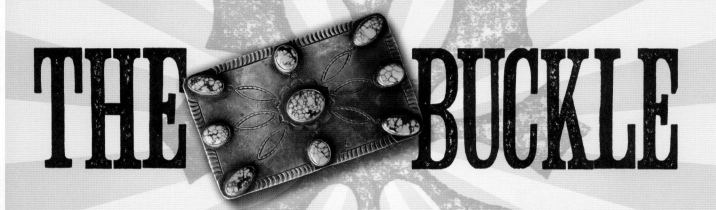 BUCKLE

Ways to hold up your trousers:

    a) bib overalls
    b) suspenders
    c) a leather belt

How your belt shows the world you're a cowboy:
leather tooling and a big silver concho or rodeo champ
buckle—so big it cuts into your gut when you sit down!

THE RANGER

The Navajos learned silversmithing from the Mexicans, who learned from the Moors. The Navajos' silver conchos inspired early buckles. Today's cowboy buckles are generally of two styles: the ranger and the trophy. The ranger set is comprised of a C-shaped buckle with a keeper or two (to keep the tail end of your belt from flopping around) and a corresponding tip on the belt's opposite end.

The trophy buckle can be rectangular, oval or practically any shape—heart, cross, star or whatever the buckle maker can dream up. It began as a rodeo prize, inscribed with the name of the rodeo, event, date and the winner's name. The pride associated with a cowboy winning a rodeo buckle is comparable to an actor winning an Oscar.

THE TROPHY

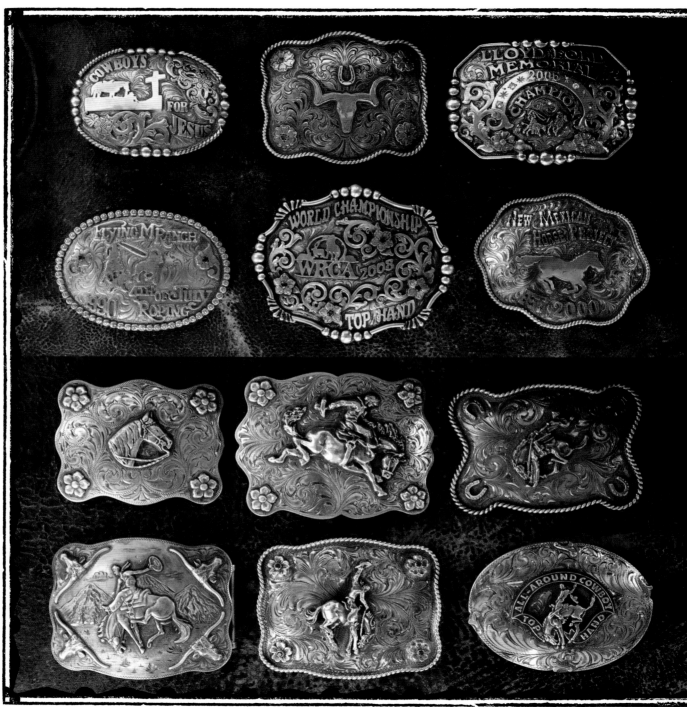

TROPHY

Trophy buckles can be the size of a silver dollar but are usually much larger—some so large you could use them as dinner plates! Is it pretentious to wear a trophy buckle if you're not a rodeo champ? Not really. As long as it is a buckle that says something about you, even if you don't rodeo. It's about the same as wearing cowboy boots if you don't ride the range, which most boot wearers don't.

CASE

Cowboys are an inspiration: freedom is their motto. To dress and look like a cowboy is a compliment to them all. The first adornment, after boots, of course, is the buckle. A buckle with flair is one of the few choices men have in the accessories department. Actually number one!

COWBOY

Buckle makers use a variety of metals, including sterling silver and 10k to 18k gold, German silver, coin silver, Damascus steel, copper and brass. Their creative imaginations in the designs and use of materials have pushed the limits of buckle making. The buckles can be accentuated with a variety of gemstones, such as diamonds, rubies, sapphires and emeralds. Designs include flowers, hearts, crosses, brands, initials, longhorns and, more recently, skulls. Older companies like Bohlin, Comstock and Vogt, have been joined by current masters Clint Orms and Silver King in creating fabulous masterpieces. These trophy buckles are so elegant they are no longer a cowboy exclusive—they complement an Armani suit worn by a business executive or cowgirl Jane's skin-tight sexy jeans. Ride 'em, cowgirl!

THE QUOTABLE WILL ROGERS

NO MAN IS GREAT IF HE THINKS HE IS

I NEVER MET A MAN I DIDN'T LIKE

JOSEPH H. CARTER ★ FOREWORD BY LARRY GATLIN

ADVICE FROM WILL ROGERS

From
The Quotable Will Rogers

ADVICE CAN GET YOU INTO MORE TROUBLE THAN A GUN CAN.

211

A MAN THAT DON'T LOVE A HORSE,
THERE'S SOMETHING THE MATTER WITH HIM.

Photo courtesy of the Will Rogers Memorial Museum, Claremore, Oklahoma.

THERE AIN'T NOTHING TO LIFE BUT SATISFACTION.

Photo courtesy of the Will Rogers Memorial Museum, Claremore, Oklahoma.

WHAT CONSTITUTES A LIFE WELL SPENT?
LOVE AND ADMIRATION FROM YOUR FELLOW MEN
IS ALL THAT ANYONE CAN ASK.

Photo courtesy of the Will Rogers Memorial Museum, Claremore, Oklahoma.

WE SHOULD NEVER REACH SO HIGH THAT
WE FORGET THOSE WHO HELPED US GET THERE.

Photo courtesy of the Will Rogers Memorial Museum, Claremore, Oklahoma.

LIVE YOUR LIFE SO THAT WHENEVER YOU LOSE,
YOU ARE AHEAD.

Photo courtesy of the Will Rogers Memorial Museum, Claremore, Oklahoma.

YOU MUST JUDGE A MAN'S GREATNESS
BY HOW MUCH HE WILL BE MISSED.

217

I NEVER MET A MAN I DIDN'T LIKE.

218

Photo courtesy of the Will Rogers Memorial Museum, Claremore, Oklahoma.

WHEN A FELLOW DON'T HAVE MUCH MIND,
IT DON'T TAKE LONG TO MAKE IT UP.

219

YOU DON'T CLIMB OUT OF ANYTHING AS QUICK AS YOU FALL IN.

THE MORE YOU KNOW, THE MORE YOU THINK SOMEONE OWES YOU A LIVING.

221

RUMOR TRAVELS FASTER BUT IT DON'T STAY PUT AS LONG AS TRUTH.

Photo courtesy of the Will Rogers Memorial Museum, Claremore, Oklahoma.

A Cowboy's Blessing

May Your Belly Never Grumble,
May Your Heart Never Ache.
May Your Horse Never Stumble,
May Your Cinch Never Break.

To my friend Johnny, who is a cowboy.

Jim Arndt is a nationally recognized editorial and advertising photographer. He maintains studios in Santa Fe and Minneapolis and shoots for clients such as Wrangler, Chevrolet, Marlboro, *Paris Match* and Harley-Davidson. His personal work has also been exhibited in galleries in Santa Fe, Taos and Austin. He is considered one of the leading authorities on cowboy boots and collaborated with Tyler Beard on *The Cowboy Boot Book, 100 Years of Western Wear, Art of the Boot* and *Cowboy Boots*. He also collaborated with Mary Emmerling on *Art of the Cross*. www.jimarndtphotography.com

ACKNOWLEDGMENTS

Thank you to all the cowboys and cowgirls who helped with the gathering of information and images in this book:

Nathalie Kent, Clint Mortenson and Wyatt, Johnny, Manuel Cuevas, Dave Little, Bob Sandroni, Marty Johnson, Tara Kent, Reggie Jackson, all the boot makers, buckle makers, hat makers and the craftsmen of all things western.

To my riding buddies Gary and Monique, Lelek and Jasmine, Amado and Ricardo.

Thanks to Suzanne and Madge for wrangling together the book.

A huge thank-you to my sister, Kathy Graves, who made all the words happen . . . I couldn't have done this without her.

And the inspiration to be a cowboy and live the western style.

Thank you to my cowgirl Nathalie, who is dedicated to keeping our Western heritage alive.

—JA